TOP 10 RICHEST ATHLETES

BY JIM GIGLIOTTI

The Child's World®
childsworld.com

Published by The Child's World®
1980 Lookout Drive • Mankato, MN 56003-1705
800-599-READ • www.childsworld.com

Photo credits:
AP Photo: Michael Conroy 4, 14. Newscom: Laurent
Baheux/Flash Press/Icon SMI 5, 12; Carl Costas/MCT/
Newscom 6; Aaron Gilbert/Icon Sportswire DES 7;
John W. McDonough/Icon SMI 500 8; David Becker/
UPI 9; Aaron Josefczyk/Icon SMI 603 10; Jim Middle-
ton/UPI 11; Anthony J. Causi/Icon SMI 942 13; Jeff
Siner/MCT 15; DPP/Icon SMI 547 Gilles Levent 16;
Gero Breloer DPA 17; Dan Honda/Contra Cost Times
18; Glyn Kirk/Actionplus Sports Images 19. Dreams-
time.com: Mike Monohan 2; Mquirk 21. Shutterstock:
Photovs (cover), 1; Goir 7 bottom.

ISBN: 9781503827257
LCCN: 2017960464

Printed in the United States of America
PA02380

CONTENTS

Introduction: Who's Number One?. 4

Kobe Bryant. 6

Roger Federer 7

Magic Johnson. 8

Floyd Mayweather 9

Jack Nicklaus. 10

Arnold Palmer 11

David Beckham. 12

Michael Jordan 14

Michael Schumacher 16

Tiger Woods. 18

Your Top Ten! 20

Sports Glossary 22

Find Out More 23

Index/About the Author 24

WHO'S NUMBER ONE?

At the end of a sporting event, everyone knows who won. In a team sport, it's the team with the most points! In tennis or golf, it's the winner of the final match. Choosing the richest athlete of all time is a bit more difficult. Is it the person who makes the most money in a year? Or is it the player who makes the most off the field? Is the richest athlete someone who made the most money in their career? Fans, experts, and fellow players all have their opinions.

Opinions are different than facts. Facts are real things. Michael Jordan was the NBA's scoring champion 10 times. That's a fact. Jack Nicklaus was the best clutch putter ever in golf. That's an opinion. An NBA playing court is 94 feet long. That's a fact. Madison Square Garden is the best place to watch a basketball game. That's an opinion.

Some people might think Tiger Woods is a better clutch putter than Jack Nicklaus was. That's fine; that's their opinion. But they can't say Nicklaus didn't win 18 major golf championships. That's a fact.

Michael Jordan

New York Knicks' fans think Madison Square Garden is No. 1. But you would find a very different opinion in lots of other NBA arenas, where fans think THEIR place is No. 1.

And that's where *you* come in. You get to choose who is the richest athlete in history. You will read lots of facts and stories about these great athletes. Based on that, what's your opinion? There are no wrong answers about who is the richest athlete of all time . . . but you might have some fun discussions with your sports-loving pals!

Read on and then after you're done, make up your own Top 10 list.

David Beckham

WE'RE #1

Bryant and his wife give away a lot of money. The Kobe and Vanessa Bryant Family foundation works to end youth homelessness.

KOBE BRYANT

BASKETBALL

In 1997, Kobe Bryant was 18. He signed his first **contract** to play pro basketball. He had just graduated high school! He would be paid more than $2 million in his first two NBA seasons. Not a bad way to start!

That was only the beginning. Over the next two decades, Bryant made an astounding $328 million. He played 20 seasons with the Los Angeles Lakers. In his final season, he turned 37. That year, Bryant was paid more than $25 million.

There was a reason the Lakers paid Bryant the big money. He was an 18-time All-Star who helped the team win five NBA titles. He was the NBA scoring champion twice, and once scored an amazing 81 points in a single game.

"The Black Mamba" was all-NBA in defense 12 times!

NUMBERS, NUMBERS

All-Time NBA Scoring Leaders

Player	Points
1. Kareem Abdul-Jabbar	38,387
2. Karl Malone	36,928
3. Kobe Bryant	33,643
4. Michael Jordan	32,292
5. Wilt Chamberlain	31,419

ROGER FEDERER

TENNIS

Federer is an Olympic gold medalist. He teamed with fellow Swiss star Stan Wawrinka to win the doubles gold in 2008.

In 2017, Roger Federer stunned the tennis world. In fact, he surprised the entire sports world. He won the Wimbledon **singles** title. That was not the surprise. It was, after all, his eighth title there. The shocker was that he did it at age 35. That's a ripe old age for a tennis pro! In fact, Federer was the oldest player ever to win one of tennis' **Grand Slam** championships.

Federer's big win was the highlight of a huge 2017 season. He added another Grand Slam win at the Australian Open. He closed the year with 95 career singles titles, second-most in the professional era.

All that winning has added up to a whole lot of money! Federer entered 2018 with more than $100 million in career earnings. Some of that money went to the Roger Federer Foundation. This group helps educate children in southern Africa and in his native Switzerland.

NUMBERS, NUMBERS

Federer's Grand Slam Wins

Australian Open	6
French Open	1
Wimbledon	8
U.S. Open	5

MAGIC JOHNSON

BASKETBALL

Johnson is big in another sport, too. He used some of his money to buy part of the Los Angeles Dodgers in 2012.

His given name is Earvin Johnson. Everyone just calls him "Magic." There's no other way to describe what he could do with a basketball in his hands.

Magic was a 6-9 **point guard**. His skill made the Lakers' famous "Showtime" offense of the 1980s go. He led the NBA in **assists** four times and helped his team win the league title five times. Magic was an NBA All-Star 12 times in his 13 seasons. Three times, he was named NBA MVP.

Magic's success goes far beyond the basketball court. He owns several businesses and donates a lot of money, too. His business skill helped him pile up more than $500 million.

In the early 1990s, Magic got the disease AIDS. To help others with that illness, he has raised lots of money and helped those seeking a cure. That might be his best magic trick of all!

NUMBERS, NUMBERS
NBA Career Assists Leaders
1. John Stockton   15,806
2. Jason Kidd   12,091
3. Steve Nash   10,335
4. Mark Jackson   10,334
5. Magic Johnson 10,141

FLOYD MAYWEATHER

BOXING

Boxers make a lot of money in a very short time. Most matches last less than half an hour. But it's a hard sport and they risk great injury. Many people love to watch and they don't mind paying.

Perhaps the most famous boxer today is Floyd Mayweather. He made more than $700 million in the **ring**. Since 2006, he earned at least $25 million for each of his fights!

Perhaps the biggest was in 2017. Mayweather had retired, but came back for one big event. He defeated Conor McGregor, a mixed martial arts champion. He took home more than $300 million from that one fight!

Mayweather fought 50 times and never lost once. He was a world champ at five different weights.

Mayweather has retired for good. He owns a company that puts on boxing matches featuring other fighters. No surprise: He makes money from those, too!

NUMBERS, NUMBERS

Most big fights are on pay per view (PPV) TV. That means fans buy the fight broadcast the way they would buy tickets for a movie. In all, Mayweather's fights brought in $1.67 billion in PPV money. That's by far the most ever!

9

JACK NICKLAUS

GOLF

In 1962, Jack Nicklaus got his first paycheck in golf. He finished in 50th place and made $33.33. For his first win later that year at the U.S. Open, he was paid $17,500. Nicklaus went on to become one of the most successful golfers in history. He won 117 pro tournaments over several decades.

These days, playing pro golf for a living pays a whole lot better! The 2017 U.S. Open winner, Brooks Koepka, earned $2.16 million. Nicklaus has a fortune of more than $1 billion. Most of it came from being a great businessman and from designing new golf courses. Nicklaus and his wife, Barbara, have been very generous, too. Nicklaus hosts a golf event that gives money to a children's hospital in Ohio.

NUMBERS, NUMBERS

Most Major Golf Championships

1. Jack Nicklaus	18
2. Tiger Woods	14
3. Walter Hagen	11
4. Ben Hogan	9
Gary Player	9

At age 46 in 1986, Nicklaus became the oldest player ever to win the famous Masters golf tournament.

ARNOLD PALMER

GOLF

Arnold Palmer was at his golfing peak in the 1960s. His many fans were called "Arnie's Army." The Army loved his go-for-broke style of golf. At every event, the Army followed him around the course.

Sometimes, Palmer's style of play resulted in spectacular victories. He captured seven major championships in seven seasons from 1958 through 1964. Other times, his style sent him to sad defeat. But it was always entertaining!

Palmer's personal appeal was enormous. Using it, he branched out into many different businesses. "The King," as he was known, wrote books, designed golf courses, and helped found TV's Golf Channel. That helped him build a huge fortune.

Ever had lemonade mixed with ice tea? That drink is called an Arnold Palmer. It was his favorite! →

NUMBERS, NUMBERS

$10 million: That's how much Palmer left in his will for Arnie's Army. That's what he called his foundation that helps children and their families.

DAVID BECKHAM

In 2013, David Beckham made $5 million in five months. That's how much he was paid by the Paris Saint-Germain soccer team. That's a ton of money to you and me. For Beckham, though, it was just a drop in the bucket. In his long soccer career, he made more than $700 million.

By 2013, Beckham was 37. He was no longer the same dominant player who starred for England's national team. He had also won titles with several pro soccer clubs.

Beckham could make a soccer ball move like perhaps no other player ever. His curving free kicks are legendary. A movie was called *Bend It Like Beckham!* after his amazing skill.

Beckham helped his teams win titles in four countries: England, France, Spain, and the United States.

Away from the field, Beckham really raked in the dough. He promoted everything from sunglasses to theme parks to underwear.

At the height of his career, he was the world's highest-paid soccer player. Over the years, he has used his money to help others, most notably children through UNICEF. That $5 million he got in Paris? He gave it all to a children's charity in France. How about "Give it like Beckham?"

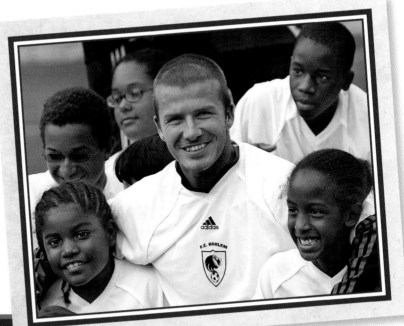

MICHAEL JORDAN

BASKETBALL

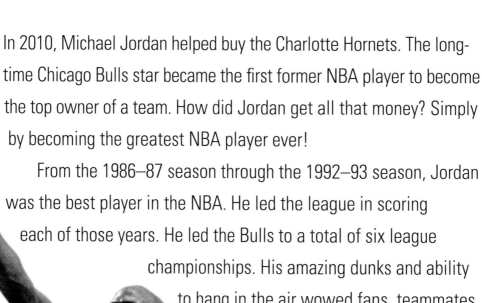

In 2010, Michael Jordan helped buy the Charlotte Hornets. The long-time Chicago Bulls star became the first former NBA player to become the top owner of a team. How did Jordan get all that money? Simply by becoming the greatest NBA player ever!

From the 1986–87 season through the 1992–93 season, Jordan was the best player in the NBA. He led the league in scoring each of those years. He led the Bulls to a total of six league championships. His amazing dunks and ability to hang in the air wowed fans, teammates, and opponents. He was the biggest reason the NBA exploded in popularity around the world in the 1990s.

Jordan's uniform number 23 has been retired by the Chicago Bulls. It was also retired by the Miami Heat—even though he never played for the team!

That success earned Jordan a ton of money. In each of his final two seasons with the Bulls, he was paid more than $30 million. Off the court, his many deals made him even more money. The biggest was with Nike. In 1985, they named the famous "Air Jordan" sneaker for him.

Jordan retired after the 2003 season. He has been almost as good in business as in basketball. Today, he is worth more than $1 billion. Jordan has been generous, too. In 2017, he made his largest single gift. "MJ" gave $7 million to medical clinics in Charlotte, North Carolina.

NUMBERS, NUMBERS

All-Time NBA Scoring Leaders
(Points Per Game Average)

1. Michael Jordan	30.12
2. Wilt Chamberlain	30.07
3. Elgin Baylor	27.36
4. Kevin Durant	27.13
5. LeBron James	27.12

MICHAEL SCHUMACHER

AUTO RACING

Germany's Michael Schumacher was one of the most successful race car drivers in history. He won the Formula 1 world title a record seven times. Racing is a dangerous business, but he survived. In 2013, Schumacher was in a bad skiing accident. He suffered a severe brain injury. Surgery saved his life. Since then, he has been in treatment.

Recovering from such injuries can be expensive. Fortunately, Schumacher made a lot of money winning all those races. He earned more than $1 billion during his amazing career.

In 2012 alone, for instance, Schumacher made about $30 million. That included race winnings and business deals. He was world famous after winning five F1 racing titles in a row, beginning in 2000!

During his racing career, Schumacher helped many world charities. He did not talk a lot about it, though. He gave quietly to UNESCO and ICM, the Brain & Spine Institute. In 2004, he gave $10 million for victims of an Indian Ocean **tsunami**.

Today, he is still recovering. The people he helped and his racing fans hope he can win that race, too.

Schumacher's younger brother Ralf was also a racer. They finished one-two in five F1 races.

NUMBERS, NUMBERS

Schumacher's Records

Most F1 Driving Championships: 7

Most Race Wins in a Career: 91

Most Race Wins in a Season: 13 (2004)

TIGER WOODS

GOLF

Golf history can be cut in two. There is the time before Tiger Woods and the time after. Thanks to his popularity, the time *after* Woods has been very, very good to pro golfers. He helped bring really big money to the sport, starting in 1996.

Woods brought golf to non-sports fans, too. He smacked booming drives. He made perfect chips. He made clutch putts. More than anything, he had a will to be the best. All that kept TV viewers glued to their sets. Golf courses he played on were packed. All those fans meant more money for all the golfers, not just Woods.

Woods brought energy to golf. After a big shot, he pumped his fist. He loved hearing the cheers after a big shot. In his **prime**, Woods owned the **majors**. He won 14 of them, second most all-time. He excelled in the World Golf Championships.

Woods's real first name is Eldrick. He got his famous nickname from his father. Tiger's dad had a friend in the Army with that nickname.

Woods's 18 wins at the World Golf Championships are the most ever. Those events also pay out the most money. So it's no surprise that Woods is pro golf's all-time money leader. Entering 2018, he had earned more than $110 million. He also made tens of millions more promoting products and in business deals.

Tiger gives a lot of it to help others. The Tiger Woods Foundation was founded in 1996. It helps children in need get to college and find other ways to get an education. It's not just pro golfers who say, "Thanks, Tiger!"

NUMBERS, NUMBERS

Tiger's Majors

The Masters	4
U.S. Open	3
British Open	3
PGA Championship	4

With 79 all-time tournament victories, Woods entered 2018 second only to the legendary Sam Snead (82 wins) on the PGA Tour's career list.

YOUR TOP TEN!

In this book, we listed our Top 10. We gave you some facts and information about each athlete. Now it's your turn to put the players in order. Find a pen and paper. Now make your own list! Who is the No. 1 richest athlete of all time? How about your other nine choices? Would they be the same athletes we chose? Would they be in the same order? Are any athletes missing from this book? Who would you include? Put them in order—it's your call!

Remember, there are no wrong answers. Every fan might have different choices in a different order. Every fan should be able to back up their choices, though. If you need more information, go online and learn. Or find other books about these great athletes. Then discuss the choices with your friends!

THINK ABOUT THIS . . .

Here are some things to think about when making your own Top 10 list:

• What sport did he play?

• Was he popular with fans off the playing field or court?

• What did his fellow competitors think about him?

• Did the athlete often win (or help his team win)?

SPORTS GLOSSARY

assists (uh-SISTZ) in basketball, passes that lead directly to points

contract (KON-trakt) an agreement that shows how much a team will pay a player

foundation (fown-DAY-shun) a group set up to give away money to help others

Grand Slam (GRAND SLAM) in tennis, the four most important tournaments: Australian, French, and U.S. Opens, and Wimbledon

majors (MAY-jurz) in golf, the four most important tournaments: The Masters, the U.S. and British Opens, and the PGA Championship

point guard (POYNT GARD) in basketball, a player who dribbles the ball up the court and passes to teammates

prime (PRYME) the most successful period of an athlete's career

retired (ree-TYRED) in this case, when a uniform number is removed from ever being used again by a team

ring (RING) in boxing, the canvas-covered square where the fighters meet

singles (SING-ullz) in tennis, one-on-one matches between two players

tsunami (tsoo-NAHM-ee) a huge flood that comes from the ocean

FIND OUT MORE

IN THE LIBRARY

Christopher, Matt. *Michael Jordan: Legends in Sports.* New York, NY: Little Brown Books for Young Readers, 2009.

Roselius, J. Chris. *David Beckham: Gifted and Giving Soccer Star (Sports Stars Who Give Back).* Berkeley Heights, NJ: Enslow Publishing, 2010.

ON THE WEB

Visit our Web site for links about Top 10 richest athletes: **childsworld.com/links**

Note to Parents, Teachers, and Librarians: We routinely verify our Web links to make sure they are safe and active sites. So encourage your readers to check them out!

INDEX

Air Jordans, 15

Arnie's Army, 11

Beckham, David, 5, 12-13

Bryant, Kobe, 6

Charlotte Hornets, 14, 15

Chicago Bulls, 14, 15

England, 12

Federer, Roger, 7

Formula 1, 16

France, 12, 13

Germany 16

Johnson, Earvin "Magic," 6, 8

Jordan, Michael 4, 14-15

Los Angeles Lakers, 6, 8

Mayweather, Floyd, 9

McGregor, Conor, 9

NBA, 6, 8, 14

Nicklaus, Jack, 4, 10

Nicklaus, Barbara, 10

Nike, 15

Palmer, Arnold, 11

PGA, 10, 11, 18

Schumacher, Michael, 16-17

Switzerland, 7

Woods, Tiger, 4, 16-17

World Golf Championships, 18

ABOUT THE AUTHOR

Jim Gigliotti is a former editor at the National Football League who is now an author. He has written more than 80 books on a variety of topics for adults and young readers, including several biographies in the popular "Who Was?" series for children.